CM 11

SID
THE KITTEN

First published in Great Britain 1989 by Andersen Press Ltd
and in Australia by Century Hutchinson Australia Pty Ltd

This Piper edition published 1990 by
Pan Books Ltd, Cavaye Place, London SW10 9PG

9 8 7 6 5 4 3 2

© Mark Foreman 1989

ISBN 0 330 31403 3

Printed and bound in Great Britain by
Springbourne Press Limited, Basildon, Essex.

SID THE KITTEN

Mark Foreman

Piper Books

This is Sid. Although he was two and a half months old, Sid never seemed to grow any bigger. He stayed small.

Not like his seven brothers and sisters. They even looked different from him. Somehow Sid just didn't fit in.

When it was time for supper with Mother, there wasn't any room for him.

He was always hungry.

And when the others played hide-and-seek around the house, Sid played alone.

He tried to get his paws on the goldfish, but the glass was too thick.

He tried catching flies, but broke a vase instead.

Chasing mice was fun, but he never caught any.

One cold night, Sid saw his mother slink home
with a fish in her mouth. She didn't offer him a bite,
and right there and then he decided to run away.

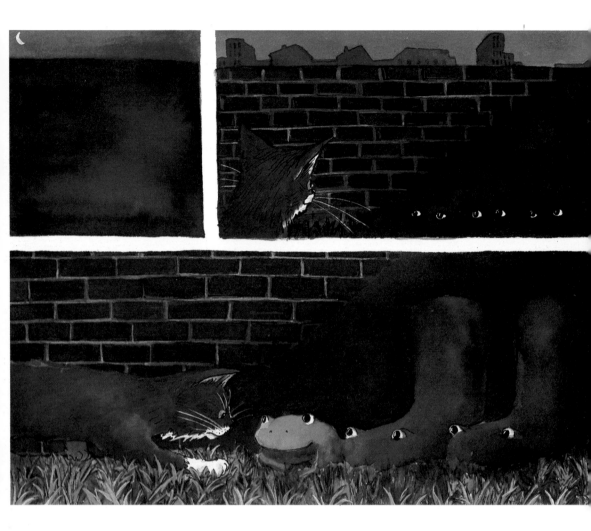

The world outside the catflap was black as soot, except for a yellow slice of moon. In the grass before him six eyes glittered. Slowly, Sid crept forward . . . and came face to face with a slimy green frog.

His hair stood on end as the frog jumped up and disappeared. Behind him there was a snuffling and shuffling.

Sid turned round. He'd never seen a hedgehog before. He didn't know how prickly they were, but he soon found out.

Away from the garden was another world, a world
of grimy brick and enormous warehouses stacked
with fish.

"This must be where my mother went," thought
Sid, as he tiptoed past a snoring guard down a long,
silent passageway. A mouse peeped round one of the
containers.

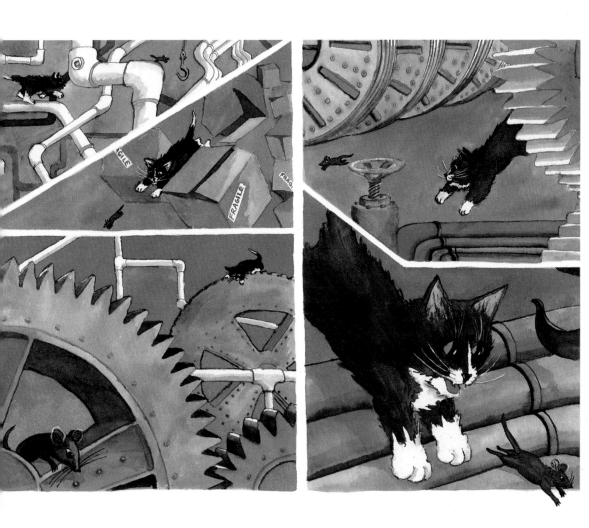

Sid didn't hang about. Down rusting pipes,
through old cardboard boxes, across huge metal
wheels he chased the mouse — but couldn't catch
him.

Fed up and panting a bit, the little cat wandered back into the night. He wrinkled his nose at the stink of rotting garbage. Then from behind some dustbins came a fearful yowl.

Caterwauling and spitting, a pack of mangy
tomcats dashed after Sid, who ran for his life —

right under the wheels of a metal monster. With an ear-shattering roar and a squealing of brakes, the lorry just missed squashing the terrified Sid.

He ran and ran until the night was gone, and as dawn rose over the grey river Sid found himself on a long, narrow bridge —

which led to an old paddlesteamer.
　　Tired, trembling, and still very hungry, Sid slipped under a chequered canopy, and closed his eyes.

He slept through breakfast, lunch and might have slept through tea . . . .

A parade of bright balloons, gripped by small hands, bounced in the air towards the steamer.

Cakes and crisps, blancmange, biscuits, sausages
and sandwiches were spread across the table.
Shouting and laughing, a horde of children
clambered onto chairs and the party began.

Sid woke up with a start. His nose twitched. Mmm! Food!

He looked up at a row of feet and streamers.

"This could be exciting," he thought, when an ice cream cone was dropped on his head where it stuck fast!

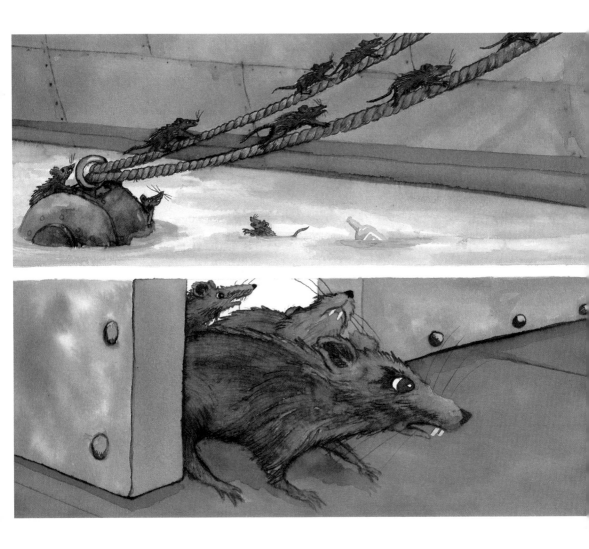

Outside, swimming through the oily water, a bedraggled rat crawled onto an anchor buoy, then another and another . . . . Up the thick ropes they scuttled.

Along the deck they rushed, and into the room where the party was in full swing.

There were screams and yells. Food scattered and shattered on the floor, to be gobbled up by the ravenous rats.

Imagine their shock when, from behind an iced cake, a demon cat with a horn on its head reared up with a terrible hiss.

The rats turned and fled. Down the ropes they dashed, tails waving like streamers.

In their mad panic to escape some toppled into the water, while Sid taunted them from the deck and the children cheered.

The party was for Sally's birthday. She was the granddaughter of the paddleboat's captain, and five years old that day.

The best present she had ever had was Sid.

"So tiny and so brave," she whispered as she cut the cake. "Do you think we can keep him, Granddad?"

"Of course, Sally. He's obviously a stray. He can be ship's cat."

That night Sid had the biggest dinner of his life, and slept in Sally's bed.

He was happy. He had a home. And maybe, he thought, maybe one day he wouldn't be quite so tiny.